Convoluted

Chinmay Chakravarty

Ukiyoto Publishing

All global publishing rights are held by

Ukiyoto Publishing

Published in 2025

Content Copyright © Chinmay Chakravarty

ISBN 9789367955277

All rights reserved.

No part of this publication may be reproduced, transmitted, or stored in a retrieval system, in any form by any means, electronic, mechanical, photocopying, recording or otherwise, without the prior permission of the publisher.

The moral rights of the author have been asserted.

This is a work of fiction. Names, characters, businesses, places, events, locales, and incidents are either the products of the author's imagination or used in a fictitious manner. Any resemblance to actual persons, living or dead, or actual events is purely coincidental.

This book is sold subject to the condition that it shall not by way of trade or otherwise, be lent, resold, hired out or otherwise circulated, without the publisher's prior consent, in any form of binding or cover other than that in which it is published.

www.ukiyoto.com

It's with a scary foreboding that I move around these days, for I've been watched! Somebody is watching my every move—some shadowy figure in black that I can't say I've discovered or have seen in person. But I'm very sure of it! I've been home for the last few days working on a special project of mine and to be with my wife who is safe with me. Don't ask me what is my project about, for I've not even told my boss in that private firm where I've been working as a data operator since several years while getting my leave for a few days sanctioned by him. Suffice would be it to say that my project is very important and rather covert. Now, coming back to the point of being watched I must tell you that in the last few days, say a week, I got out of home only two or three times during which I had a hunch that somebody was tailing me from home to the places I visited or recced. However, I was not very sure of it, because I couldn't manage to spot my mysterious follower or followers.

But this evening as I plan to move out on a crucial part of my project, I'm almost sure of it, for I seemed to have spotted a figure in black fleeting from under a street light post in front of a small shop to a waiting car where another shadowy figure in black dress sat tight and stooped over the wheel, the moment I slightly drew the curtain in my living room to have a view so as to confirm my worst fears. Probably the guy under the light post became aware of my peeping-out and to perhaps assuage my doubt went to the waiting car and got inside, and possibly instructed the driver to move away as the car indeed started moving—to make it conclusive for me, I think.

I stuck to my observational post and watched how far the car had gone from my house. Indeed! It disappeared round the bend—maybe about two hundred meters from the front side of the building where I own a two-room flat with my wife. But I knew for sure the car must've stopped after rounding the bend and one of the guys must still be looking out for my movements. My foreboding and the sighting, however, failed to dissuade me from going out on my mission, if I could term it that way, for the simple reason that this is the crucial part as I'd already mentioned to you. And besides, I can very well go on living with my worries or tensions or forebodings or whatever, I can tell you that. Is there any soul on planet earth who is so blissfully rid of any of these? Impossible!

By the way, my wife also works as a lecturer in a junior college of the sparkling city that we live in. We got married seven years back and combining our resources we applied for a home loan thanks to which I finally could purchase our dream home—in a respectable housing society and in a more or less prime locality too. It's been two years since we moved in to our own flat. We bought a small family car in the second year of our wedlock.

For the last few months we've been discussing, brainstorming and speculating about making a baby. For me it's just the right time, for I've been confirmed in my position in the private firm while there was no possibility of my wife losing her far more secure job of an educator. But my wife loves to debate everything—howsoever small or utterly insignificant the matter could be—and this being a serious life-defining matter she's taking her time. I allow her that freedom. Our decision about having a baby, therefore, is pending at this particular moment.

True to her sincere and dedicated nature, my wife is always loath to leaves of absence from her teaching job unless there's an emergency of sorts; however, on this particular occasion I succeeded in persuading her to join me in our project which I told her is far more important to her than to me. I further told her that these few of days of living together would do a world of good to both of us in fulfilling our joint-mission in life, apart from the oft-repeated but facile excuse of spending some quality time together. And, she's been really happy and safe with me the last few days.

My decision of going out that particular evening having been sanctioned with the seal of my own authority, I threw a flying kiss to my wife who'd been sleeping soundly for quite some time now which she is used to term as a brief power nap though, and moved out.

I deliberately chose to exit from the farthest wing of the residential block which is also the farthest point from the direction of the car that moved away. Once out on the street I hopped into a bus rather than hailing a cab which is my usual option, going in the opposite direction of my destination. This would, I'm sure, put them off my tail unless, of course, they are pros in their job. The point of my followers being pros suddenly makes me think harder. Why would professionals try to spend so much time in following me around, considering the plain fact that I'm only a small fry doing my most mundane jobs or keeping the most ordinary errands? And pros or not, why would anyone tail me around at all? Who are they and what is their purpose or objective?

As quickly as it came to my mind, I dismissed it. Why should I bother about something that I won't be able to understand by all possible means at that particular moment? I had better concentrate on my present job which requires me to put them off my tail as soon as possible if they were indeed following me around so that I can accomplish my task without unwanted interference and possible sabotage. And that was exactly what I did.

I got down from the bus after about four or five stops and hailed a cab, still sticking to the opposite direction to that of my intended destination. To make doubly sure I asked the cabbie to stop before a sprawling posh restaurant cum bar, and settling the fare I entered from the main entrance. I chose a table at the corner along the glass wall so as to afford me the widest possible angle to view and explore the frontside of the bar that obviously had the busy road with incessant traffic. Relieved to find no suspicious objects or movement there I ordered a pint of beer, all the while looking at my wrist watch which told me not to waste more time than necessary if I wanted to keep my appointment at the destination I recced at least two times before, I think I told you that already.

After finishing my beer and paying the bill, I took a last look outside: no! no car nor the shadowy figures there to be seen. Still, to be on the cautious side, I took permission from the manager to allow me to exit from the rear door. Therefore, I marched through the kitchen that finally led to the private exit. Hitting the road that ran almost parallel to the one where I landed from the cab, I started walking along the pavement—this time in the direction of my destination.

I was just about to hail a cab when a frightening thought struck me. I stopped in my tracks to ponder over the issue: now that they've been put off my tail what they'd do in the professional way? How likely are they to find my destination on their own? I'm not sure about that, for I was not convinced that they followed me there on those two or three occasions; although a distant possibility remains, I can somewhat safely rule that out. What then? The next thought was scary.

Yes! They'll drive back to my house where my wife is—no longer safe without me! They may possibly force their entry into our house to interrogate my wife about my whereabouts! The absolute lack of information about the quality and quantity of my stalkers could mean undefined and thus more pronounced danger for her!

I became very anxious and tense. That foreboding in my mind became more than real now! There is another detail that I haven't mentioned so far, but maybe only indicated, that in the recent days I've been constantly haunted by an image. The image of a large tattooed hand belonging to a tall bearded brawny man pulling my wife away from me—she struggling to look back at me again and again, her eyes terror-stricken and wide imploring me, beseeching me to be brave and come forward to rescue her! Before I come to know of what action I should take or have taken the image vanishes! And this detail has heightened my sense of danger to a huge extent, so much so that I entered a store and asked the desk guy's permission to use the landline phone. I offered money too. The guy, probably sensing my anxiety and my somewhat decent manners, allowed me to do so, dismissing my offer of money with a smile.

My hands trembling, I dialed my wife's mobile phone and on being connected I immediately began my sermons without waiting for her to air her usual queries: 'Please do stay indoors till I come; don't answer the calls if the numbers are not recognized; don't respond to the doorbell rings, and never ever open the door to anyone—I insist anyone; put off the house lights, and if you're still feeling sleepy sleep on, till I come! Please understand, darling! … okay, goodbye!'

Maybe I should've carried my cell phone along. I stopped taking the phone with me on my outings since the last few days as a security measure. I know very well that mobile-tracking makes the shadowing job much easier and more convenient. In these happening times, not just the investigators or the criminals, but every Tom, Dick or Harry knows how to track smartphones and other electronic devices. Therefore, I think, my decision is justified, particularly on such a crucial day as today.

Happy that I could warn her in time, I walked out thanking the store guy and took a normal black-yellow cab that was standing there. I told the cabbie about the place I wanted to visit. The place was in the midst of the crowded streets of the central parts of the city, dominated by both new-age high rises as well as the dilapidated old blocks, whereas we live in the suburbs which are highlighted by mushrooming high-rise housing societies and many more under construction.

It took me around two hours in taking the roundabouts in order to put the stalkers off my tail, but as my watch indicated I was still on time. It's been my constant habit to set off for an appointment much earlier than required as per traffic conditions, and this habit has paid me rich dividends on this important day too. My hands that trembled a lot minutes before are now workably steady.

I ran a last-minute check all over my body—taking stock of all the objects that I was carrying—the objects that were absolutely necessary for what I aimed at accomplishing that evening. Everything is in order, I assured myself.

All the while on the ride I'd also been watching and checking all activities around—on both sides of the road and the rear. No suspicious cars, nor stalkers, nor followers, nor shadows. As the raid parties usually sound off, I too told myself 'All clear'!

Suddenly I felt a bit unwell and weak. In fact, I've been having a bad headache and a burning sensation in my body since morning accentuated by palpitations now and then. Sitting in the taxi now I was acutely aware of my heart starting to beat faster, and that unpleasant numbing sensation running through my arms to the fingers. As my irritation kept growing because of these most unwelcome symptoms, those haunting images staged a comeback making me think about the meaning or significance of all that.

Why? My wife has always been safe with me. As well as all the women in my family—mother, sisters, cousins, school friends and all—have been safe with me thanks to my efforts to ward off dubious company or even friends. Of course, I cannot stay on at a single place to be around with the ladies there, and apart from the instructions and guidance rendered there's nothing I can do about it if anything untoward happens.

Therefore, is this a reflection of that deep-seated fear in perhaps every right-thinking male that some rare circumstances or some unexpected twists could lead to some cowardly crimes, thus endangering their beloveds or even snatching them away? Such predators, such perverts are everywhere nowadays and they could be anybody—known and unknown. I often wonder why it's a common practice to not invite the wives to the liquor parties of male colleagues or friends! Not because, I say, women normally don't prefer alcoholic drinks or don't prefer to sit in drinking parties, but it's because we the males don't know or can't predict our potential behavior under those circumstances with countless pegs inside our bloodstream. I became very concerned and anxious for my wife's safety now. "Goddamn sickening motherfuckers!" I exclaimed aloud.

The taxi driver looked back, "Hello Saab! Are you feeling, okay?"

That only increased my irritation. "Not your fucking concern! Mind your own driving!"

The offended driver concentrated on the road ahead fully now, mumbling, "Sorry Saab! I was only a bit worried!"

I felt sorry for him, but said no words in consolation. I used that incident as a means to steel my nerves for the upcoming appointment: control the mind and thus apply full control of the body—its muscles, the pulse, the burning, the flushing and everything. For me this appointment holds absolute significance in finding possible solutions to the problem of the predatory vultures infesting our society.

"Please stop the taxi here, bro!" I said to the driver in a very polite tone now.

"Okay Saab! But your address is still some distance off!"

"Yes, I know! I'll have an evening walk!"

I paid and thanked him and moved away in the direction of the address.

It was about ten in the night which is not at all considered a late hour in the city, especially in these busy parts. There was steady traffic, lots of people on the streets and inside the restaurants and bars.

I decided to keep a slow steady pace, for I was determined to keep my mind and body calm and composed. After about five minutes of walking I took a left turn into a by-lane which was relatively darker thanks to the far-apart and the weaker street lamps, in sharp contrast to the brilliantly lit main busy road. The third residential block, quite an ageing building, on my left was my destination.

As I neared, I could clearly see the black Xylo parked under a big tree, a few yards away from the building entrance. I slowed down further and crept up to the vehicle which, I knew, was occupied at the driver's seat.

I knocked softly on the window of the door on the passenger side. The opaque glass slid down instantly and the bulldog-like face of a short burly hairy man stared at me suspiciously. Very soon his face broke into a distorted grin as recognition dawned on his fearsome face. "Why man! You seem to be that fucking joker! What would you possibly want with us now?"

"It's urgent! Just a word if you don't mind, buddy!" I whispered.

"As you please, asshole!" he unlocked the door. I opened it, eased in and occupied the passenger seat.

"What's it, shithead? I heard things…!"

"I wanted to show you something important!" I put my left hand into my trouser pocket as he eyed me, half in curiosity, half in jest. "No shit! How could I even think of confronting you guys?" I assured him as I began withdrawing my hand.

What happened next was even quicker than what I guesstimated about the seconds it was going to take for the full plan put in action.

I capped his mouth with my right hand while my left, in the meantime, succeeded in taking out and opening the blade of a knife. Without yielding him time to react or to anticipate I held the sharp and pointed blade upward and drove it through his neckline, maybe just above the thyroid gland, and moved it up and up with a force that surprised me—never thought my rather lean and thin body would be able to exert that much force.

The utterly astonished man's hands flayed wildly—his left trying to gnaw at my face and his right aiming for the horn at the steering wheel. I pinned down his left hand with my knees as I nearly rode on him while with the elbow of my striking hand, I prevented his right hand from reaching the steering wheel. It was accomplished in only a few seconds during which not a sound escaped through the man's vocal cords except for a horribly suppressed gurgling—howsoever tough he supposedly was.

The spurting blood dismayed me temporarily, generating a wave of nausea inside. It was everywhere—bursting through his torn jaws and throat, bleeding from his mouth, his nose, his ears and even through his insanely widened blazing eyes. I gulped down my saliva a few times and was able to control the churn in my belly, fully concentrating to keep my clothes clean of the oozing-bursting-cascading red stream. And I kept on thrusting the knife up and up, till his body became limp and still.

I pulled the knife out, wiped the handle with my handkerchief and threw it disdainfully on his lap. After wiping my palms and putting the napkin back in my pocket I clutched his back hair and shoved his head down on the steering wheel and also pulled his hands putting them on both sides too. I checked my dress in the weak stream of light that filtered through the windshield. Thanks to the precautionary steps I took there was not a single blood stain on my blazer, shirt and on the trousers. Giving his loathsome body a feverish and a deliriously elated last look I quietly opened the passenger door and alighted, instinctively looking around.

There were people standing, sitting on the pavement and inside parked cars, but nobody heard or saw a thing as to what happened inside the Xylo. They didn't even notice me as I walked away from the back of the car to the block I wanted to visit.

I reached the building entrance and as I entered a watchman probably in his late sixties trying to find as much comfort as possible on the wooden stool put up against the brick-exposing dirty wall, directed a weary look at me, yawned and waved me inside.

I climbed the spit-infested stairs and the corners up to the third floor. I paused in front of the flat where I had the final appointment and put my right hand on my back, under the blazer. With my left I pressed the doorbell hard.

A sound emanated from the inside. "Who's it?"

I allowed myself just a grunt which I made as rough and ugly as possible.

"Is it you, Raghu? What brings you here, fucker? Anyway, just a minute!"

Presently he opened the door a crack, and his face changed to incredulity as he beheld me in front. "Whoa! Poor fish! How dare you come here?" a tall tattooed bearded brawny guy barked at me. Beholding him there, no longer a haunting image but a reality now, put my blood on boil. Composing my words in as cowardly a voice as possible under the circumstances I rather croaked, "Hi and sorry boss! I have a very urgent matter to discuss with you!"

"Why didn't you speak to Raghu first, fucking idiot? he's down there in the car!" said he and was about to close the door. I put in quickly, "I spoke to him boss! And he really did listen! He thinks it's better I put it up directly with you! It'd take only a minute!"

"But why didn't the bugger accompany you?" he hesitated, but finally waved his hands up, perhaps observing my cowering and seemingly helpless frame, and opened the door. Such was his overconfidence that he started walking with his back turned to me. "Make it quick! I've to go out!" he was heading for the teak-wood sideboard placed against the wall on my left to probably have the last sip from the glass lying there.

"Just a minute, boss!" I uttered in the coldest of tones I was capable of delivering.

He turned around and his face immediately took on a perplexed look as he found me with a gun pointed directly at him. His hands by his sides quivered visibly, perhaps trying to grab something or anything nearby.

Like I did before, I denied him the extra seconds to react properly to the singularly peculiar situation as far as he was concerned.

I shot him at the groin, the bullet tore through the part of his hateful body that he probably always considered the most essential one. A hideous shriek came out even as with his right hand he started groping the sideboard, maybe trying to open the top drawer.

I shot his right hand at the shoulder joint. This time he crashed to the floor, toppling the glass and the whiskey bottle from the sideboard. I watched the poisonous blood flowing freely from his wounds as he struggled to rise again, using his left hand as support.

I walked up to him, put a bullet in his left hand too and pressed my foot upon his groin, pressing as hard as possible. His groans now issued with lesser and lesser intensity. And I shot him pointblank at the center of his chest.

I'd have gone on putting bullet after bullet into his frightfully strong sinews had I not heard a commanding voice from the doorway.

"Lower your hand and put that fucking gun on the floor! Quick or I'll shoot!"

I beheld a man in black that I instantly recognized as one of my stalkers. I gave a long sigh of satisfaction while following the instructions.

"Now, come forward, kneel down on the ground and put your hands on your back!"

"Who the hell are you?" I demanded as I continued with the instructions dutifully.

"Why should you fucking bother?" the man in black retorted as he handcuffed me from behind and picked up the gun while issuing instructions on his smartphone. "Homicide! I need backup! Also send the forensics!"

Relaxing on my knees I stared at him and remarked sarcastically, "well, well! You must be then from the police! Beats me! How on earth you thought it worthwhile to follow an ordinary citizen around?"

The policeman gave me a contemptuous look. "Ordinary citizen? No! you're a bloody murderer and a criminal! You just shot down a man dead and you try to sound so casual, unrepentant!"

"Two!" I announced proudly.

Now it was his turn to stare at me! "How do you mean?"

"Instruct your companion to check the black Xylo parked under a tree below!" I teased him further.

The policeman barked the order to that effect, and a short while after got a call back. He listened and grimaced. He looked at me with plain incredulity. "My God! You very much look a decent man, with a moderation-defined frame and most probably with a white-collar job. How can you even think of committing such barbaric crimes?"

I made a statement. "These are bad people. They did harm. They should be killed like this, and if you guys don't do your duties, we citizens must take up the axe!"

"What harm have they done and to whom? Your wife, your sisters, your relatives?"

I shouted at him now. "You're all compromising shitkickers! Why it has to be always your own people wronged to think of some action? All citizens happen to be your own people, don't you agree? Then why you never do anything substantial? Always listening to your political masters or the rich and the powerful and protecting them at any cost, instead of protecting us the ultimate victims?"

My words seemed to have a pacifying impact on the policeman. "You've to work within a system and observe the rules. Like you citizens we too cannot take law into our own hands."

"Fuck the system if you can't turn it around ever! And for your information, apart from being rapist-murderers these two goons are also drug peddlers, racketeers, high-profile pimps and protected by their political masters. Don't you know about them? You follow me around, instead of investigating such criminals!" I cried out.

"We regularly launch campaigns against all such criminals, but the malaise has of late become so widespread that we don't have enough manpower and facilities to tackle it effectively." He made his best effort to justify, clearly much against his wishes—like having a conversation with a criminal who just brutally murdered two guys instead of shooting him down on the spot.

I was beginning to think now that he was basically a good man. "What's your name, if I may know!" I asked.

"Why not! You'd know a lot of me soon enough! I'm Inspector Bhaskar. Pleased to meet you, sir!" some of his arrogance and sarcasm hissed through this time, justifiable by the plain fact that I was the criminal caught red-handed at the crime spot.

At that moment several policemen along with the forensic experts entered the house. And a thorough examination began.

"So, obviously you're going to arrest me, no?" I inquired politely.

Bhaskar grimaced, "What do you expect, dude? You commit a brutal double-murder, and you muse about getting arrested?"

"No! I ask for a different reason! Please inform my wife of my arrest and custody. She must know!"

"What wife?" Bhaskar asked casually.

"Hey! Don't you dare insult a lady in that tone of yours! She's not a commodity to be addressed that way! Call her up and if you get her voicemail give her the message anyway. At this hour she must've exhausted herself waiting for me and gone to sleep possibly!"

"But we took a look before catching you here. There was no response to our repeated rings and loud knocks on the doors and even windows! No one seems to be there! luckily, I remembered you coming into this lane in one of your previous visits."

I felt vindicated and thought, oh! You acted as I thought you'd!' Then I said aloud, "no! I gave her instructions to behave that way, for I didn't know my followers were policemen! And I still don't understand why policemen should be after me!" I added after a thought, "but how even to trust policemen nowadays?"

Inspector Bhaskar moved a few paces away from me dialing his phone. He talked for some time and I couldn't catch a word he said, notwithstanding my best straining efforts.

After supervising the examination of the crime spot for a few minutes Bhaskar came to me asking me to get up. "Please help me to stand on my feet! As you can clearly see, with my hands cuffed behind my back I cannot possibly do that on my own." I protested.

He went behind me and put his hands under my arms to support. The moment I achieved a standing position I felt enveloping waves of dizziness, seeing the stars dancing before my eyes, my stomach churning with an obnoxious charge of nausea submerging me and my knees buckled under me. I nearly blacked out and was only dimly aware of several people assisting me to a chair. Before I could feel the comfort of sitting down on a chair I fainted.

*

When I came to, I found myself on a hospital bed instead of what I feared would be the cement floor of a dirty police lock-up room. I felt drowsy and weak. I noticed the cap on my left wrist that obviously connected to the saline fluid bottle above. As I looked around, as if through a mist, I found it was the general ward of a government hospital and it was rather well-maintained and clean despite the tag. Moving my eyes around I saw Inspector Bhaskar talking to a man in a doctor's uniform. I could pick up the words now of the conversation that must've been going on for a while.

"So, Doc! You're sure he's not faking the illness?" Bhaskar asked.

The doctor shrugged his shoulders and replied, "definitely not! As I told you already, he must've had a terrible shock recently, and he's been living the trauma the last few days—accentuated by I think prolonged sleeplessness, no proper meals and absolutely no care of self. When he was brought here, he was running a very high fever too, and I'm sure the fever must have been on him for at least the last two days. Besides his mind remains foggy, and although I'm not a psychiatrist I can say that it seems he's been blocking his mind from something surfacing!"

The inspector looked at me and finding me focused on them, he asked, "but at the moment he's conscious and seems to be following our conversation. Can I speak to him now?"

"You can try, but I'm not very sure of results."

Bhaskar bent over me resting his hands on the edge of my bed. "Where is your wife?"

I stared blankly up at him. He repeated, "Where's your wife? Tell me!"

I found my lips rigid, and so I whispered through them, "She's safe with me!"

"What did you say?" he leaned forward putting his ears to my lips as closely as possible.

What issued from me was at best a mumbling, "she's safe with me!"

The inspector stared at me in a very awkward and perplexing way. The doctor came up to him at that moment. "I think you had better let him rest for the night. He's under strong sedatives, and he must get some strength back to think and speak. Come tomorrow morning, he should be relatively sound and alert by then."

"Okay, Doc! I'm putting two security guards outside the main door. Inform all your staff not to allow any visitors under any circumstance. For anything untoward you have my number. Thanks!

*

Bhaskar was back at my side the next morning, occupying the chair offered by the attending nurses. I was propped up into a more or less sitting position by the nurses, wheeling up the headboard of the steel bed. I was feeling much better after eating a breakfast which, however, I found to be absolutely tasteless and bland. I looked at the inspector and indicated with a wry smile that I was ready for his questions.

"Where's your wife?" he began exactly from where he left.

With annoyance surging up within me I replied, "I already told you she's safe with me!"

"What do you mean by that?"

"I mean what I exactly meant by that! As long as I'm there she's going to be safe, always!"

"But you're not with her now! And she wouldn't know when or if at all you get the bail order!"

"She's not an ordinary lady, mind you! She's a thinker, teacher and a doer, you see! And she does understand that I'd be by her side wherever she is or wherever I am."

"Cut out the crap, and tell me what happened!" the inspector became visibly impatient and angry now. "And I must tell you that last night I sent a team to your flat. There was no response from inside and not a single light was burning in any of the rooms. So, as per my instructions, they broke into your flat…!"

I stared at him frostily, interrupting him with my equally cold retort. "Whoa! That's pretty highhanded, I suppose, apart from being illegal! Without my filing an FIR about my wife missing or something you can't do that!"

"Don't teach me how police should work! There's a lot of suspicion about your wife's whereabouts, and you must know that her college principal tipped us about her: that her mobile phone had been continuously on voicemail since the last few days and that she hadn't informed the college about her absence from work!"

"So you decided to put a tail on me?" I knew now why I thought I was being followed.

"Precisely! Now back to the point of your flat being broken into. Your wife was not there, and the team found only her mobile phone. After going through the phone here in our computer room…you know what we found?" he gave me an intriguing look. I looked back at him as impassively as I was capable of, and waited. "There are several voicemail messages including quite a few of your own! You calling your wife on voicemail from various landline phones! Why would you do that? How do you explain that?"

"Okay! I've put her up in a safe house by my own standards of safety! And you know! I love her passionately…so much so that I just can't continue without speaking to her now and then, every day! It's been a habit since I fell in love with her during our college days." I paused and exhaled a long sigh. Bhaskar had been focused on me, in an incredulous sort of way. "And you'd understand, I never wanted her mobile with her to compromise her security. So, I kept the phone on the bed we sleep on!"

"But why would you put her in what you call a safe house which is normally used by us and other security agencies?"

I hit him back with a ferocious look now. "To protect her from the goons I killed!"

The inspector leaned back on the chair as much as the chair would allow, in total bewilderment and disbelief. "Oh! So, you tell me you wanted to kill them before ensuring full protection for you wife! What do you think the police are here for, huh? Why didn't you file a report and ask for our protection? All policemen are not corrupt and sold out as you think!"

I smiled at him now. "Then how on earth would I have been able to rat them out and kill them?"

"Okay!" the inspector sized me up in not a very appreciative way. "You're a man of medium height with a somewhat frail body, no? and completely nil experience in this field! How the devil you were so confident that you'd be able to eliminate them the way you did?"

"I think I have the intelligence and brains. You see! You need not always engage your ominously physical targets into fisticuffs to overpower them, you can find some other way to accomplish that! The element of surprise is very important here!"

He gave a questioning look and I continued. "Like you observed just now, they also considered me useless and harmless, a coward as they addressed me. But apart from the intelligence I mentioned, I do work in a field of endless possibilities—the internet you know! With the minimum of information available about the goons I succeeded in tracking them…"

"What information did you have about them?"

"Their car number which was actually a fake, but it provided me with crucial leads like their confirmed political connections; their faces that are so permanently etched in my memory and I used those to find their identities, their possible police records and their probable places of dwelling! Further, I have contacts in your own department, apart from in various other investigative agencies—pals who benefited from my expertise and so who always help me out without asking too many questions!"

Bhaskar perhaps thought at that moment what I'd been thinking all the time that he'd so far not asked me the most obvious question. So, he decided to fulfil his curiosity now. "But what started your kill-kill project? I mean what led you to plan it out? Any prior violent incident?"

"Yes, something happened which for us was never a violent event. It was simply a case of road rage!"

"Tell me all about it!" he commanded. So, I told him.

*

That cloudy evening while returning home in our car I picked up my wife from her college as she was having a late class; we then visited a grocery store for the essentials and was on our way home. At a busy traffic signal, I stopped the car even as the lights turned red and waited. One SUV in front of ours that didn't keep the proper lane discipline took the road on the right, thus creating an empty space. The moment I moved our car ahead to fill that space, another SUV behind us on my right also moved ahead, aiming for that empty space. And our vehicles brushed one another before stopping for the signal to turn green.

The short hairy stocky man with the face of a bulldog at the wheel grimaced and grunted at me blabbering continuously. I immediately lowered my window glass and pointed out that his vehicle moved suddenly without any sort of a signal, but I said sorry anyway. The staccato burst of words didn't stop though, and it was even made worse by the muscular bearded giant with tattooed hands occupying the rear seat joining in the rant, the latter commanding us to stop after crossing the traffic point.

We looked at one another. My wife told me to say sorry again and also say that fortunately no harm was caused to any of the vehicles involved. I did so, and as the lights turned green, I moved the car accelerating to the normal speed in due course.

To our extreme irritation as well as apprehension the other vehicle followed with the brawny giant waving at me repeatedly to stop the car. I too waved at him indicating it was not necessary, and moved on.

The SUV suddenly increased its speed and overtaking us it swerved to the left blocking our way. Both of the ominous looking fellows got down, moved to my side and started lambasting for not heeding their call to stop.

I got down and asked them to examine the cars. If there was a slight scratch in the right bumper of our car, there was nothing at all in theirs. However, the bulldog-faced one happened to discover a spot and said it was caused by the friction. I maintained that the spot must've existed even before the cars touched to which the brawny tattooed man protested, assuming ominous tones now.

At that point my wife got down and joined the debate, trying to safeguard me from the wordy tirade; she soon took the lead and pointed out the faults in their arguments while emphasizing the point again and again that both the cars were unscratched and thus there was actually no scope for further arguments. The goons were in no mood to relent and I failed to understand what exactly they wanted from us.

By that time a motley crowd assembled there and many of them began taking the side of my wife—obviously finding a damsel in distress with the loudmouth goons about to heckle her physically.

Finally, the crowd won the case for us. They threatened the goons in no uncertain terms to get into their car and get the hell out immediately or else they'd call the police. With sullen and scowling countenances, the short and the muscular men left the scene, and the crowd booed them out. We thanked them profusely and left for home, rather disturbed though.

Back home I dwelt on the incident for quite some time, and concluded that we couldn't ignore it as a mere case of road rage, for I pointed out to my wife that the two guys looked really ominous and were probably criminals. My wife fully agreed to my proposal to find out more and more information about them.

*

"So, you decided to knock them off for that mere incident? Just like that?" said Bhaskar in plain disbelief. He was the farthest from being convinced of my story.

"Not exactly, inspector! As I told you I first researched on them and discovered them as dangerous criminals!

I got very much concerned for my wife, and for scores of other vulnerable women. So, I packed her off to a friend's house out of the city where nobody would be able to find her, including your network!"

"Okay, I do confirm that they were dangerous criminals, and in a way, you've done a service to us neutralizing them! But they have a huge network and ideally you should help us cracking that!" the inspector looked at me rather sympathetically now and added, "however, you're not doing anything to help your case. You must produce your wife with her corroborating story, and in that eventuality the courts might take a sympathetic view of your acts. You see, at this particular moment, you too are not above suspicion. Who knows you may as well be involved in some way in the supposed disappearance of your wife!"

I stared at him coldly. "Yes! What else can you do! Apart from always victimizing the victims or survivors further!"

This time it was with absolute pity that he looked at me and left.

I indicated to a nurse to lower the headboard of my bed. And I lay full-stretch on my belly, dug my head into the pillow and cried and cried and cried, wetting the pillow to its depths.

No! the last part of my story I narrated to the inspector was a lie! I was not at all disturbed by the road rage incident; in fact, I was elated at my wife's oratory and arguments winning the support of the common people on the road and congratulated her on the way back home and again there. yes! We or rather I didn't take the incident seriously and forgot about it in the coming days and weeks. It's my mistake! A grievous irreparable one at that! I won't be able to forgive myself ever again! I must go on suffering for that! My love, you're very safe where you are! I'll never compromise on your dignity! Never!

At that moment the attending doctor's team came in. I hurriedly turned my pillow on to its other side, so as to hide the impact of my tears and lay ready for their examination. I was subjected to an elaborate examination following which the nurse came straightening the headboard up as the lunch was ready. I could hardly eat anything, not because the food was bland and tasteless like the previous meal, but because my mind was in turmoil—the things that I didn't allow to come back to torment me since the last few days came flooding back, moistening my eyes—the tears that came back like a cloudburst just moments ago.

I finished eating as quickly as possible, in order to not draw attention from those present in the ward and to not being reported upon, indicated to the nurse to again lower the headboard and resumed my previous position of lying on my belly digging my face into the white smoothness and crying. Even as the final chapter of my miserable life rushed in.

*

Out seventh marriage anniversary fell on that Sunday, about three weeks from the road rage incident that we never really recollected, particularly not on that special day that we planned to celebrate with spirit and aplomb.

We drove out early in the morning, moving to the greenest district of the state, out of the concrete and grime of the city. We drove in joyful abandon through the beautiful two-lane cemented highway, lined with lush green dense forests on both sides.

We breakfasted heartily at a food-plaza on the way. Around noon we landed up at a famous fort that we couldn't visit in our years together. We strolled around chatting and joining our arms most of the time. Then there were the snaps and selfies with our mobile phones, and the occasional calls that my wife made to friends and relatives or the calls that came to her and to me wishing both of us on the special day.

We then drove to a resort, about ten miles from the fort, and had an elaborate lunch—replete with all the delicacies we both preferred. Then we lounged out in the armchairs in the huge garden and had our evening tea there. It was nearly dusk then and we thought it was time we left. My wife told me to drive non-stop and that we ought to have our supper in a favorite restaurant in the city, much nearer home.

It was about nine in the night when we reached the stretch of the highway with forests lining up both sides. At that hour the forests looked pitch black, and since there were no street lights the road got illuminated only when other cars approached and passed. The traffic was sparse.

Presently I beheld an SUV, probably a black Xylo, in the rear-view mirror bearing fast down on us. I slowed to let it pass. It didn't do so and slowed down too. A bit alarmed I increased the speed to which the car behind also responded similarly. I then told my wife. She observed the scenario for some time and asked me to stop at a convenient spot so that the car pass us by.

We stopped with the headlights on. The car behind seemed to be passing us, but as soon as it did so, it suddenly swerved to the left ahead and stopped too. The road rage incident suddenly came to my mind like a flash as I thought I recognized the vehicle. I got very alarmed and scared now.

Before we could do anything like racing away which in fact appeared to me as the most reasonable course of action, the driver and the rear passenger stepped down from the car. The driver drew out his gun immediately and shot down the two front tyers of our car. My wife shrieked in genuine fright. I realized now the best course of action we should've followed was no longer available, and I began cursing myself loudly and never stopped doing so till my moments in the hospital, while assuring my wife in a voice that I myself couldn't believe in, "Don't worry, darling! Stay composed and calm. Everything is going to be alright!"

The short stocky hairy guy with the face of a bulldog came to my side pointing the gun squarely at my head while the tall bearded tattooed brawny man accosted my wife on the other side, yanking the door open. He then started pulling my shrieking wailing begging wife out of the car in front of my own eyes. I couldn't move as the gun now touched the right temple of my head. In an unbearable agony gnawing at both my body and soul I howled expletives as well as pleadings, hoping for some other cars come by or the occasional police patrol coming by for our rescue. Nothing of that sort happened. One vehicle did pass us, but the driver or the passengers if any never looked our way. "Quiet! Else both of you die, first your darling wife!" hissed the hairy goon, breathing down my back.

I sat helpless as I watched my pleading wife being pulled and dragged away toward the vehicle parked ahead—occasionally she managing to take a look back at my direction with her eyes lit by the headlights of our car beseeching me to come to her rescue. Unable to do anything I fervently hoped nothing wrong was going to happen to her.

The hairy goon's gun was lowered then caressing my chin and sliding to my neck region. "You see! My boss is usually very rough with ladies in general! But the women like yours who dare to insult him or shout at him get the capital treatment and mostly they never come back! So, you had better bid her a warm farewell lest you never see her again!"

"But why …why… why? What have we done?" I mumbled, stumbled and gurgled, and to utterly no avail as the gigantic dwarf only laughed like a hyena.

The brawny goon pushed my wife into the back seat and then signaling the other he got in too. I could no longer hear her again or even see her as she must've been pinned down on the seat immediately.

The hairy dwarf moved away from me, went to the rear of the car first putting bullets into the rear tubes also. Then he sneered at me again, "rot, you coward! Go home and cry to your heart's will! Right?" and then he grinned from ear to ear, "maybe sometime later you gotta get married again! Ha, ha, ha!" with that he walked briskly up to the Xylo, started the engine and drove off.

In a mad rush I ignited the car and crushed the accelerator to the limit, but the poor thing issued only a horrible grinding sound moving a few yards ahead and then sopping. I threw the door open, got out and ran after the disappearing car. I wept I wailed and waved wildly at a passing car that obviously didn't stop. I sat on the hard cement floor of the road, I laid myself down full stretch on it and then sitting up, and went through the process again and again and again. Exhausted and traumatized I then got into the car, putting my head down on the steering with violent sobs coming up through the heavy lump in my throat. I saw her purse lying on the rear seat, her phone inside vibrating. I picked it up, pressed it into my bosom and wept, letting the calls go unanswered.

A few passersby discovered me inside the car early morning, nursed me back to my senses pouring water over me. They also made me drink a little. I ignored their questions and kept mum all the time. Finally, they hailed a bus headed toward the city, lodged me inside and wished me well. I looked at them tearfully, thanking them silently.

The pain got only worse as I reached my empty home. I closed all doors and windows, lay down on the bed and sobbed and wept and wailed, not caring lest it be heard by the neighbors who hardly ever existed for us all the time anyway. Still, something called hope lurked in my heart, that she'd come back to me, that she'd get released by the demons finally and that I'd shower on her all my love and take the maximum possible care to restore her damaged body and soul to normalcy.

*

My tortuous reverie got interrupted as Inspector Bhaskar made his appearance, accompanied by the doctor.

"Look mister!" he said to me. "Doctor says you're more or less okay now, except perhaps for your feeble and rather uncooperative mind. Therefore, we'll take you tomorrow morning and produce you in court. With the case at this stage, we'll ask for police custody for at least ten days and we'll get it for sure. The police lock-up room is not going to be as comfortable as this, I'm afraid!"

I nodded at him silently without exposing any emotion.

"I ask you again, despite your inexplicable indifference. Please ask your wife to come out and make your case stronger. Else it's bound to get only worse; I assure you!" he looked at me incisively.

"Don't ask me that again, sir!" I replied angrily. "I'll never compromise her in public, you take that as final from me!"

"How do you mean public? Her identity will be kept a secret, and I personally assure you that we'll protect her in all possible ways."

"Yes! Very correct! You can ensure only personally! But the ones interested will discover her identity in a jiffy! And I don't want that! I don't want her to be discussed in public or be given a fearless name by the media! In particular, I don't want my beloved wife to be pried open by the prurient vultures in social media!"

"Oh God! How very stubborn you are! Can't you see reason at all! Every such incident also creates an awareness, gives warnings and creates movements!"

"I know that! But to what avail? A movement starts in a big way, then peters off! Till one of our women get savaged to provide another incident so that another movement can start, and so on! Do you know the basic blunder behind all such public awakenings? I tell you!

Because all such movements look upon the governments to come forward and protect them! No! governments can never protect them, it's practically impossible. For the system within each government will never allow it to do what's right. It's with us only, if we change ourselves in some way!"

"But you know that your way in this particular case is very wrong and illegal! This is never a solution!"

"I know that! My method is wrong indeed! But what else can we do?"

Exasperated, the inspector strode away from me toward the exit. Before going out he threw perhaps a last straw at me wanting me to catch it before it left me. "You know what? All your concerns for your wife may go in vain ultimately! For the simple reason that in that so-called safe house she might very well find out about you from the newspapers or the television channels and may very well decide to fight for you! Don't tell me you've insulated her from all such modern means of communication too!"

I smiled weakly at him and bade him goodbye. And my inner voice rammed against my heart, 'you fucking idiot! Why don't understand she'll never come back? She's been dead for the last seven days, you condescending nincompoop!'

In the evening of the day I came home after leaving my wife in the clutch of the demons I received a few photographs in my mobile phone from an unidentified number. I immediately rang up the number, but there was a message of it being no longer in use. It must've been a burner sim. A deadly chill ran down my spine as I saw the photographs—kind of a chill that I can't explain like some sensation of an unknown disease that cannot be explained to a doctor howsoever one tried, kind of a chill that I never thought I'd ever experience.

The photos contained images of the utterly devastated and indescribably mutilated body of my wife taken from various angles. It was no longer the face I so dearly loved to watch on with its varied expressions—from heavenly smiles to fake anger and more; it was no longer the body I always adored and dreamt of it bearing our child. Her eyes that always rained down love and love on me now looked fixatedly above—at something that she could no longer behold, something she could no longer fan her beautiful eyelashes at.

My tortured mind wondered, why at all they had to do this to my wife? What was her fault or mine or ours? Beautiful person that she is, she always loved debates, always loved to argue out a matter thus possibly arriving at a solution! Was that her fault?

This time I didn't sob or weep or wail. An anger of an immensity I was never aware of started taking possession of my soul— like the anger of a raging bull, like the anger of a wild dog with its prey eluding it, like the anger of a growling tiger imprisoned in a cage.

With anger came a resolve. And whatever I narrated in the first part of my first story told to the inspector has been very true, although my mind never worked as a sane and structured element, for I did exactly that, researching out the demons, tracking them down, doing recces in their dwellings in order to find their daily habits and finally the planning to kill them dishing out the surprise element in splendor to benumb them before wiping them out from the face of the earth.

Sitting propped up on the hospital bed now I growl like the tiger in a cage, 'this damn sure is going to be the final deterrent that you all goddamn motherfuckers have been waiting for! Be warned, o' demons! Don't ever think I'm done and finished! I'm going to rise again and strike again and again! No! this is not just hope! This is a certainty!'

I really hold the inspector guilty for cutting short my project and mission in life. I want to tell him, 'Had you not caught me at the killing grounds and held me back I would've gone as per my plans to another city where a horrible crime took place that nearly equals my wife's in barbarity, to track down the perverts and kill them one by one. And then to many other places where the perverts are still holding sway…yes inspector, as I agreed already with you, this is very wrong and illegal, but you and your system failed to provide me with any other option!'

I smile sweetly at the nurse coming to my side to take off the bandage from my wrist. I look up at her as if saying in so many words that I'm ready to undergo the ordeal for the sake of my dear wife, and that I'm not going to perish, I'm going to rise again, and strike and strike and strike for you all. Come what may!

And by the way, I still preserve the last photos of my wife, but to discover those one has first to find my mobile instrument hidden well somewhere in my flat. I preserve those as a means to some end, who knows what may turn up in my thorny path! And not because I miss my wife and would want to behold her at any future point of time. As I've been saying all the while 'she's safe with me, will always be'!

***

About the Author

Chinmay Chakravarty

Chinmay Chakravarty is a professional specialized in the creative field with over four decades of experience in creative writing, journalistic writing, media co-ordination, film script writing, film dubbing, film & video making, management of international film festivals and editing of books & journals. Started career with a stint as a freelance journalist and then joined the Indian Information Service during 1983-2019. Writing since his school days he has published over ten books through Notion Press, Ukiyoto Publishing and Amazon KDP. Hailing from Assam he lives frequently in Mumbai and in Kolkata.

www.ingramcontent.com/pod-product-compliance
Lightning Source LLC
LaVergne TN
LVHW041557070526
838199LV00046B/2021